HEPZIBAH

Peter Dickinson

Illustrated
by
Sue Porter

Hepzibah is awful.

(It's not the right word, really. The King of Corumba once held a competition to choose the right word for Hepzibah, but nobody could suggest anything awful enough. So the King just said she was awful and gave himself the prize.)

What's so awful about Hepzibah? Everything. She eats soap. She never goes to bed, but hangs herself up by her feet from a beam in the roof and goes to sleep like that. Some days she eats soap until the bubbles come out of her ears. Last summer she broke a leg and had to go to hospital, but even there she made the nurses hang her up every night by her good leg.

She keeps a cow in the bath.

When people pass under her window she drops things on them, either cornflakes or little tiny sheep. Then she calls out "Funny time of the year for snow!" as if the people were too stupid to notice that the snowflakes were brown and crackly, or else they baa-ed. The sheep are so light that they don't hurt themselves when they fall. Usually they eat up the last lot of cornflakes and then go back to Hepzibah.

Why do they go back? Why does the cow stay in the bath? Nobody knows, but Hepzibah does seem to get along with animals. Some people say that this shows there must be some good in her somewhere, but others say it only shows how stupid animals are, not to notice how awful she is.

(I won't go on about the different ways in which Hepzibah is awful. If you like you can make a list –anything you put in it will probably be right.)

The main thing is that Hepzibah likes trouble. If there is trouble going on, she enjoys it. If there isn't, she makes it.

2124570

Of course there are a lot of stories about Hepzibah. This one is about the King of Corumba and the ice-cream and the helicopter and the dangerous smell and Mrs Evans and the bed with caterpillar tracks.

Would it make it simpler if I told you who these people are?

The King of Corumba. I don't know if he's really a King. Hepzibah says he isn't. She says he's really a gangster who got rich by swindling another gangster called Tiger O'Kelly, and he's hiding here under an assumed name. She says there's no such place as Corumba, but I don't think that proves anything. She once told me that there's no such place as Africa.

Anyway the King lives on the top floor of a tall hotel and he's made a garden on its roof, which is flat. The garden is full of the flowers of his native country. They look like buttercups to me. He has a butler called Francis Francis, who is tall and pale and stiff, but has a fine deep singing voice.

The King is rather rich and rather mean. He knows he ought to be generous, and sometimes he is, but if you watch closely while he's being generous you can see it hurts. Of course Hepzibah understands this very well, and she loves making the King give her things when he doesn't want to. Francis Francis never lets anybody up onto the hotel roof unless the King says they can come. That means he doesn't see a lot of people so he doesn't have to be generous very often. The King's hobby is inventing new flavours for ice-creams.

What's in that safe? (Shhh.) A spare crown, a bundle of letters signed "T. O'K." and a bag packed with useful things for someone who might want to run away suddenly.

Mrs Evans. She is extremely pretty. Every morning Mr Evans pushes her bed across to the window and she sits there all day, looking out. There's nothing wrong with her, except laziness. She has a lot of pretty hats, and she always wears one when she's sitting at the window. Mr Evans makes them.

Mr Evans used to be a carpenter, but now he's a hatmaker. Other women saw Mrs Evans sitting there and thought "If I had a hat like that I'd look as pretty as Mrs Evans," so he found he could sell as many hats as he could make, including the ones Mrs Evans had got tired of. Of course Hepzibah never wears a hat. Sometimes she covers her hair with a bright green scarf, and ties its corners so tight under her chin that you can see the shape of her ears through the green stuff.

The bird in the cage is a Crested Dodder. It nests in wellington boots, lays dark blue eggs and sings bass. Mr Evans made the cage like that so that it could get out and fly away, but it doesn't seem to want to.

The story begins here.

It begins one day when the King of Corumba invented a new ice-cream, mostly sardine but flavoured with honey and ginger, and decided to try it on Mrs Evans, because Francis Francis threatened to leave if he had to sample the King's ice-cream. Hepzibah looked out of the window and saw the pair of them coming, the King first and Francis Francis walking behind, carrying the ice-cream in a cornet the size of a flower-pot.

"Taking ice-creams to Mrs Evans, is it?" she muttered. "I'll soon put a stop to that."

She leaned out of the window and shouted "Come and have some breakfast, King."

The King couldn't believe his ears, partly because it was three in the afternoon, and partly because Hepzibah had never, ever offered anyone anything before. Just to see if it was true he came into the house.

"You're just in time," said Hepzibah. "I've finished milking the cow."

Smiling, she showed him into a room where he found a cow standing in a bath with milk up to its ankles. Hepzibah shook a few packets of cornflakes into the bath – the sort she normally kept for throwing. Then she took a spoon out of her pocket and handed it to the King.

"Funny time to want breakfast," she said, and went out, locking the door.

In the street the butler, Francis Francis, was standing and looking anxiously at the ice-cream. It was a hot day. Hepzibah came softly out into the road with her camera and took a photograph of him.

"Your ice-cream is melting," she said in a helpful voice.

"Madam, I know," said Francis Francis.

"You'll have to eat it," said Hepzibah. "There's a law against letting ice-cream melt all over the road. Or if there isn't there ought to be."

"Madam, the taste makes me ill," said Francis Francis.

"Poor fellow," said Hepzibah and took another photograph.

"Why are you taking photographs of me, madam?" said Francis Francis.

"Evidence," said Hepzibah. "To show the judge. At your trial."

Francis Francis began to eat the ice-cream, starting at his elbow, which was where it had melted to. Hepzibah watched him for a while, then went back into the house to let the King out of the bathroom. She was surprised to find the cow standing on the bathmat and the King in the bath, washing himself with a huge cake of soap which Hepzibah was keeping for her supper. (The cow had eaten the cornflakes and the King had let the rest of the milk out, down the plug.) Hepzibah was furious.

"Your butler is eating your ice-cream," she shouted. "I've got photographs to prove it."

"No!" shouted the King.

He jumped out of the bath, only half washed, so that he was still two different colours. He wrapped a towel round him and rushed into the road, where he found Francis Francis looking rather ill.

The whale in the picture is a friend of Hepzibah's called Big Toby. She met him when she was bathing at Truro and invited him to stay, but he hasn't come yet.

"What did you think of it?" he cried. "Too much ginger, hey?"

"Not at all, your Majesty," said Francis Francis.

"Great, great," said the King. "I knew you'd get the taste in the end. Now come on home. There's a mutton and marmalade ripple you've simply got to try..."

He ran off up the road, still wearing the towel.

Hepzibah wrote out a bill for $2,345 for soap, wear and tear of bath, hire of cow, etc. She dressed the cow in the King's clothes and drove it to the hotel but Francis Francis was too ill to answer the bell, so that wasn't any good and she went home. She had used up all her cornflakes in the bath, and the sheep were away visiting, so there was nothing to do except hang herself up from her beam and go to sleep and dream she was a crocodile.

When Hepzibah decided that the King wasn't going to pay her bill she sent him a letter. It said "To whom it may concern. When a person gives another person breakfast, then the second person ought to invite the first person back. If he doesn't, HE IS NOT BEING VERY GENEROUS! Just a hint from a nameless well-wisher."

The King read the letter and groaned.

"She's not nameless," he said. "She's got a perfectly good name. But I suppose I'll have to invite her. I wonder what soap ice-cream tastes like."

When Hepzibah got the invitation she wrote another letter.

"Dear King, it is kind of you to ask me to luncheon, but it would be more *generous* to give me a helicopter. Then I could drop in on you whenever I liked, without having to bother poor Mr Francis."

The railway is the Hepzibah and District Steam Locomotive Company. It is quite successful, although sometimes the engine-drivers strike for more cheese.

The King and Mr Francis discussed that letter for eight hours. Mr Francis said that the best thing would be to find another hotel to live in, on a different side of the world, but the King had a better idea.

Two days later Hepzibah got a very large knobbly parcel. She opened it and found it was full of bits of bamboo, with a few pieces of machinery and odds and ends. There was a note from the King saying it was a Corumban helicopter. The instructions for putting it together seemed to be written in Corumban.

Hepzibah kicked the pieces round the floor for a while, then went next door and found Mr Evans.

"You can do something useful for a change and put my helicopter together," she said.

Mr Evans loves to be helpful, even when people talk to him like that, so he came round and started work. Hepzibah didn't help at all, apart from ordering him about and telling him he was doing it all wrong, but slowly the machine took shape. It wasn't a helicopter, but it was certainly something.

Mr Evans dragged it out into the road to fit the final bits, but before he had finished Hepzibah said "That's enough, or I'll be late for lunch with the King." She leaped into the driving seat and pulled the largest lever. The machine started to tremble and buzz.

Hepzibah's cats are called Thing and Otherthing. Thing is the big one. He often looks cross, but in fact he's only worried. Is Hepzibah a Good Influence on Otherthing? Will the mice get lazy, going everywhere by train? That's the sort of stuff that worries him.

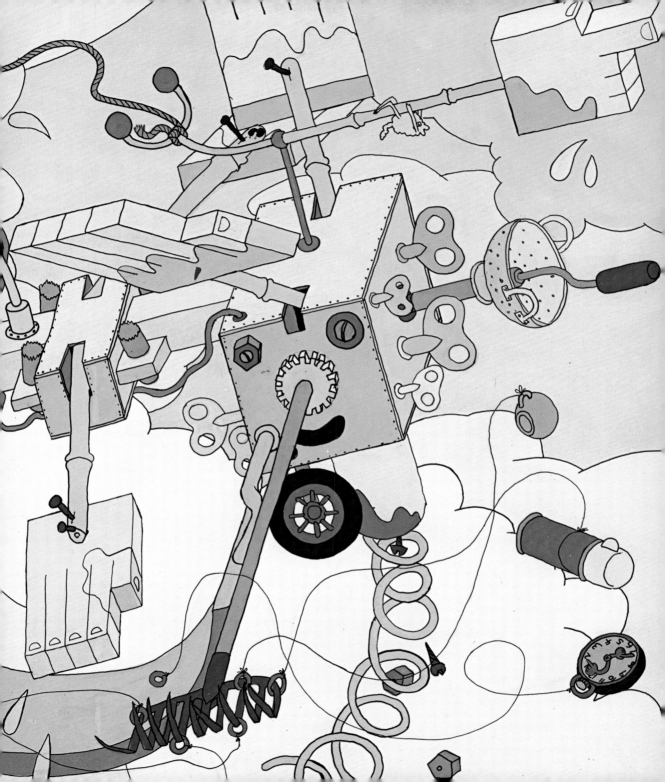

Mr Evans ran home and hid under his wife's bed.

Hepzibah pulled two more levers and the machine moved. A long bit whirled round and came down, hitting the ground with such a thump that it bounced the machine into the air, with other, shorter bits flapping and jerking. It came down just in time for the long bit to be coming round to thump the ground and bounce the whole thing into the air again, higher than before. And the next bounce was higher still.

Mrs Evans, watching out of her window, counted the bounces to her husband, who was still under the bed. There were nineteen in all, higher and higher and higher, the last one well above the roof-tops. The nineteenth time it came down the thump was so tremendous that the houses shook, and the road cracked from side to side, and the machine fell to pieces.

But the long bit was still thwacking round and Hepzibah was holding onto it because it was the only thing left to hold onto, so it shot her high into the air, far higher than any of the bounces. She came down on the roof of the King of Corumba's hotel.

That was how she broke her leg, the time she had to go to the hospital where the nurses strung her up at night by the other leg. She also made the King of Corumba bring her a soap ice-cream every day, and sit by her bed-side while she asked him questions about Tiger O'Kelly. She said he was lucky not to be in prison for sending people dangerous helicopters. Of course he knew that Kings don't get sent to prison, but still he was frightened enough to bring her the ice-creams and sit by her bed-side. He wouldn't have done it for any other reason, not even to look generous.

The first thing Hepzibah did when she got home was to telephone the council saying there was a dangerous smell coming from the cracks her helicopter had made in the road. Two lots of workmen came from different bits of the council, and they dug two holes in the road without consulting each other, and put red lamps round the holes, and then they got into their vans and drove away. That was why Mr Evans was riding on the pavement when Hepzibah threw the cornflakes at him.

What was Mr Evans doing? Well, while Hepzibah was in hospital Mrs Evans complained that life was dull and nothing happened in the street outside, so Mr Evans decided to liven things up.

Three or four times a day he would put on his crash-helmet and his leathers and his goggles and get on his motor-bike and ride down the street at 50 mph with a red rose between his teeth. As he passed his own house he would toss the rose through Mrs Evans's window. It made him feel dashing and romantic, and Mrs Evans was always interested to see whether he hit anything. Sometimes he did, sometimes he didn't. The day Hepzibah came out of the hospital he hit the King of Corumba. He can't have been expecting the cornflakes.

Nobody knows why the King of Corumba was standing on the pavement, just there. Hepzibah says he'd fallen in love with Mrs Evans and was singing a Corumban love-song under her window. Other people say that can't be right, because Corumban songs are all terribly sad ones, about old men falling off bridges. Anyway, Mr Evans didn't see the King because of the cornflakes, and Mrs Evans didn't shout to warn him because the engine of his bike made so much noise and besides she was interested to see what would happen.

What did happen was that Mr Evans made a perfect throw with the rose and the next moment his bike knocked the King of Corumba flying into the air. Mr Evans fell off the bike and his goggles and crash-helmet fell off him. (He hadn't fastened them properly because he was only going for a short ride.)

The bike knocked some of the red lamps into the hole where the dangerous smell was, then charged on by itself, straight through Hepzibah's front door. The flame from one of the red lamps set the dangerous smell on fire.* The flames went whooshing up from the hole, and the explosion knocked Mr Evans over just as he was getting to his feet. That's how he managed to catch the King, sort of, just as the King was coming down from being knocked into the air by the bike.

*This is the most extraordinary thing about the whole story—there really was a dangerous smell. It's much more like Hepzibah to make men come and dig up the road when she can't smell anything at all.

Everybody except Hepzibah and Mrs Evans was a bit dazed for a while. The King scrambled to his feet and saw a hole in the road which looked like the remains of a bomb explosion. He saw Mrs Evans looking extra pretty with the excitement. He felt it was a good moment to say something brave and generous.

So he helped Mr Evans up and said to him "Sir, you have saved my life. A villain on a motorcycle has thrown a bomb at me. It is a plot by another villain called O'Kelly. But you have thwarted it. How can I reward you?"

Mr Evans had always dreamed of saving somebody's life, and he was even more dazed than the King. Otherwise I'm sure he would have said that he didn't know anyone called O'Kelly and it had been him on the bike. But there was the King shaking his hand, so he said the first thing that came into his head.

"I'd like caterpillar tracks on my wife's bed, so that she can get about a bit."

"Done," said the King, seeing it was too late to say anything else. "I'll send my man to measure the job up to-morrow."

And he strode away, muttering about Tiger O'Kelly.

Firemen came and stopped the flames and workmen came and mended the gas pipe and filled up the holes, so there was something for Mrs Evans to watch. But Mr Evans saw Hepzibah's thin hand beckoning from her front door so he went in and found his bike lying there on its side, still roaring. He stopped the engine.

The workman in the middle of the picture is Mr Terry Dale. He is quite a good workman, honest and strong, but unluckily he is rather easily hypnotised, which slows him down.

"Now you must teach me to ride it," said Hepzibah.

"Ride my bike!" said Mr Evans.

"Or I'll tell the King," said Hepzibah. She showed him the goggles and the crash-helmet she'd picked up in the road. Mr Evans quickly became undazed. (Hepzibah does that to people.)

Next day Francis Francis came down in his overalls and started work on the bed. It took him a week. Mrs Evans moved into the spare bedroom where she could watch Hepzibah having bike lessons in her back garden. Mr Francis did a clever piece of work, so that the bed could go up and down stairs as well as along flat places. When it was finished he steered it down into the street and went back and fetched Mrs Evans, who was wearing her newest hat.

A crowd gathered to watch and cheer.

"This, madam", said Francis Francis, "is the start lever."

At once Mrs Evans pushed the lever he was pointing at. The engine purred and the bed sped off down the road.

"Hey!" said Mr Evans. "You didn't show her how to stop!"

"Madam did not give me time, sir," said Mr Francis.

"I'll never see her again!" cried Mr Evans.

"Don't be a ninny," snapped Hepzibah. "I'll fetch her back."

She rushed into her back garden, started the bike and roared off down the road, wobbling from pavement to pavement. Everyone else stood around and waited. Some of them said it was a pity to lose such a pretty woman as Mrs Evans. Some of them said it wasn't so bad if it meant losing Hepzibah as well.

They went home to lunch, then came back and waited.

They went home to tea, then came back and waited.

They were just thinking of going home to supper when, far down the road, an object came into sight. It came nearer, and nearer, until it was perfectly obviously a bed, with caterpillar tracks. Mrs Evans was driving, and Hepzibah was sitting at the foot of the bed, where Mrs Evans's cat usually sits.

"Did you have a good time, my dear?" said Mr Evans.

"Yes indeed," said Mrs Evans. "We went to London and I looked at every hat-shop, and I didn't see a single hat as nice as the ones you make for me."

Mr Evans was so happy when she said that that he quite forgot to ask Hepzibah what she'd done with his bike.

They wouldn't all look so pleased if they could see Hepzibah's face. That's the way she looks when she is planning something. I don't know what, but when I see Hepzibah looking like that I invite myself to stay with my aunt who lives in Bogota.

That's the end of the story, unless you want to know what happened to the bits of the helicopter. Nobody could fit them together again, so Hepzibah stuck them in her garden to grow beans up. The beans do very well. They are pink and crinkly and they don't taste like anybody else's beans.

The End